FROM THE CHAIRMAN

STEVEN SPIELBERG

Dear Reader:

In your hands you hold a gift.

Perhaps you knew this already—you bought this book for your son or your daughter or for a good friend. But what you probably didn't realize is that in buying *The Emperor's New Clothes*, you've also given a gift to seriously ill children. The proceeds from the sale of this book benefit the STARBRIGHT Foundation and help give back to these children what they so often lose to their illness—the freedom to just be *kids*.

Most children in hospitals are scared. Talking with them, I've found time and time again that they desperately want to know what's happening to them. Helping these kids find answers to their questions about disease and giving them creative ways to cope with the challenges of serious illness is what STARBRIGHT is all about. When kids understand what's going on and their minds are actively engaged, their lives—and often their health—improve.

STARBRIGHT's projects are remarkable collaborations, uniting the finest talents from the worlds of entertainment, pediatric health care, and advanced technology for a common goal: to give seriously ill kids a helping hand in fighting their diseases. By giving back the laughter and hope that no child should live without, STARBRIGHT helps kids overcome their pain, fear, and loneliness—and allows them to hang on to their childhoods.

This unique retelling of Hans Christian Andersen's "The Emperor's New Clothes" is yet another remarkable collaboration. It is the result of the generosity and talent of twenty-three celebrities and twenty-three acclaimed illustrators who opened their hearts to donate their time and creativity to help STARBRIGHT.

And thank you for your part in supporting STARBRIGHT's important work. All of us involved with this very special book hope you have as much fun reading it as we did creating it.

All my best,

[signature: Steve Spielberg]

Steven Spielberg

Chairman

P.S. *Beware of clever weavers!*

FOR FURTHER INFORMATION, PLEASE CONTACT:

The STARBRIGHT Foundation

1990 SOUTH BUNDY DRIVE, SUITE 100

LOS ANGELES, CALIFORNIA 90025

1-800-315-2580

http://www.starbright.org

The Emperor's New Clothes

Hans Christian Andersen's

The EMPEROR'S NEW CLOThES

An All-Star Retelling of the Classic Fairy Tale

Harcourt Brace & Company

NEW YORK   SAN DIEGO   LONDON

Liam Neeson

Harrison Ford & Melissa Mathison

Angela Lansbury • Nathan Lane

Jason Alexander • Dr. Ruth Westheimer

Madonna • Carrie Fisher & Penny Marshall

Melissa Joan Hart • Jonathan Taylor Thomas

Jeff Goldblum • Dan Aykroyd

Robin Williams • Geena Davis • Calvin Klein

Rosie O'Donnell • Fran Drescher

Joan Rivers • Steven Spielberg

Gen. H. Norman Schwarzkopf

John Lithgow

ILLUSTRATED BY

Quentin Blake • Maurice Sendak

Peter de Sève • Etienne Delessert

C. F. Payne • Mark Teague

Steve Johnson & Lou Fancher

Daniel Adel • Carter Goodrich

S. Saelig Gallagher • Gary Kelley

David Christiana • Chris Van Allsburg

Berkeley Breathed • Kinuko Y. Craft

Steven Kellogg • Tomie dePaola

Michael Paraskevas • Fred Marcellino

Don Wood • Graeme Base

William Joyce

Requests for permission to make copies

of any part of the work should be mailed to:

Permissions Department, Harcourt Brace & Company,

6277 Sea Harbor Drive, Orlando, Florida 32887-6777.

HARCOURT
BRACE

Additional material written by Karen Kushell

The publisher wishes to thank Storyopolis for sharing

our vision and for their collaboration in bringing this book to print.

Library of Congress Cataloging-in-Publication Data

Hans Christian Andersen's The Emperor's New Clothes:

an all-star retelling of the classic fairy tale.

p.   cm.

Summary: Andersen's classic fairy tale retold from

different points of view by twenty-three celebrities

and depicted by twenty-three illustrators.

ISBN 0-15-100109-X

ISBN 0-15-100436-6 (BOOK AND CD)

[1. Fairy tales.]

I. Andersen, H. C. (Hans Christian), 1805–1875.

Kejserens nye klæder.

PZ8.A542Em   1998

[Fic]—dc21   97-32021

PRINTED IN MEXICO

First edition

A C E F D B

A C E F D B (BOOK AND CD)

STARBRIGHT would like to thank the following people,
whose generous time, support, and talent made
The Emperor's New Clothes possible:

Karen Kushell
SENIOR PRODUCER

Fonda Snyder   Dawn Heinrichs
PRODUCERS

Gilles Wheeler
STORY CONSULTANT

Paul Allen

Susan Amster

Kristy Cox

Robin Cruise

Dan Farley

Michael Farmer

Anthony Gardner

Tracy Hargis

Jacquie Israel

Cheryl Kennedy

Marvin Levy

Christina Lurie

Kristie Macosko

Kevin Marks

David Nelson

Gang, Tyre,

Ramer & Brown

Jody Patton

Rubin Pfeffer

Susan Ray

Stanley Redfern

Eric Robison

Margie Rogers

Peter Samuelson

Richard Schmitz

Steven Spielberg

Michael Stearns

Peter Stougaard

Lawrence Weinberg

Frank Wuliger

...and David K. Haspel, whose idea to create
a celebrity fairy tale to benefit STARBRIGHT
inspired this book.

The Emperor's New Clothes

I WAS BORN CURIOUS.

MOTH ILLUSTRATIONS BY QUENTIN BLAKE

YOU MIGHT EVEN SAY I'M NOSY.

Okay, I'm a snoop. That's why I'm so glad I'm a moth. I'm small, barely noticeable, and I've had the chance to flutter around the world and see everything.

Well, I *thought* I'd seen everything…until I landed in an empire not so far away, where once upon a time there lived an emperor with a passion for fashion. Nothing made the Emperor more happy than wearing fancy new clothes and showing them off to everyone in the Empire.

It was soon to be the Emperor's birthday. For the parade in his honor, he wanted the most magnificent suit ever created, made from the finest materials in the world.

The best cloth in the world? How could any self-respecting moth pass up the chance to get a taste of that? I buzzed over to the Empire as fast as my wings could carry me, touching down just as the Emperor called his Prime Minister to the Imperial Palace for a "very important" meeting.…

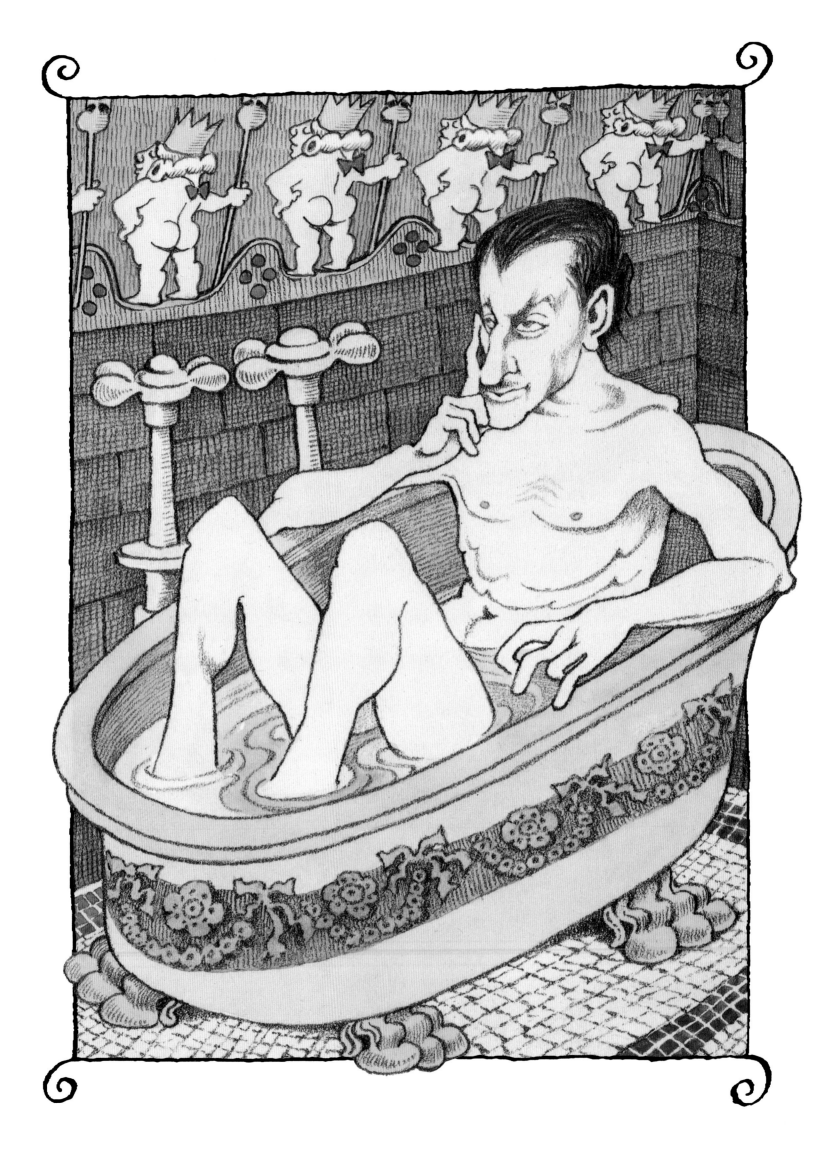

The Imperial Prime Minister

As told by Liam Neeson

ILLUSTRATED BY MAURICE SENDAK

MY OLD SCHOOL CHUM, the Emperor, is so brave, so wise, so...(*sob*) totally *wrong* for the job! It should be me, *me*, ME. I run the Empire! He's just a clothes-loving pinhead. If just once he'd say, "Cedric, I'd be lost without you," I'd be happy...or at least less inclined to steal the Empire's money behind his back. But no, it's always, "Cedric this" and "Cedric that." For instance, the vexing matter of his birthday suit.

I was busy preparing for the Summit of Kings when the Emperor sent for me. "Trusty Cedric," he commanded, "stop everything and give your full attention to finding a...*spectacular* ensemble of clothing for me to wear in my birthday parade."

Shopping? This was beneath me! I suggested he call upon one of my lieutenants, or his *wife*, for goodness sake. But he insisted *I* was the man for the job. I was humiliated...and mad. I went to take a bath, which always helps me scheme— I mean, *think*.

Soaking in my tub, looking at my wrinkled, pink body, I was struck by an idea: What could be more embarrassing than getting the Emperor to walk among his subjects NAKED...all the while believing he's clothed in the latest fashion? They'll think he's crazy and demand that he step down...then I'll take over—and finally get what I deserve!

B ᴜᴛ ᴛʜᴇ Pʀɪᴍᴇ Mɪɴɪsᴛᴇʀ couldn't carry out his evil plan all by himself. He prowled the darkest corners of the Empire in search of expert help...and found the perfect rotten accomplices.

The Weaver Thieves

As told by Harrison Ford & Melissa Mathison

ILLUSTRATED BY PETER DE SÈVE

ME AND JOHNNY was kind of on the run, see, having just scammed a wealthy stupid family out of their jewelry.

Things was fine till a nosy policeman recognized the bleeding ring on Mary's finger as belonging to some old duchess, and locked us up. Just when we thought we was goners, this pompous little Prime Minister creeps up and makes us an offer:

He'd keep us out of the Imperial Dungeon if we could get the Emperor believin' we was able to weave a cloth so fancy that stupid, tasteless people couldn't see it.

Anybody who'd hire a weasel like the Prime Minister couldn't be too hard to fool. . . . So me and Johnny, we decided to take the job.

The Emperor was putty in our hands. We told him what a fine figgur of a man he was, so handsome and refined—
"For an elegant man like yerself," I told the Emperor, "I'd advise a humble, modest line. Don't want to flash the commoners too much."

Yeah, we buttered him up real good so we could hit him up for the things we'd need: gold, silver, jewels . . .
"But nobody can weave with just minerals and gems," I said. The scam had to sound kind of genuine. So I asked for pricey silk from Chinese worms, and leaves from a tea plant in Darjeeling, India.

We was back in business all right—robbing the Emperor blind!

9

The Spinning Wheel

As told by Angela Lansbury

ILLUSTRATED BY ETIENNE DELESSERT

WHEN WORD UNSPOOLED round the palace that these Weavers had a special talent for makin' cloth visible only to them what's got taste and smarts, I was eager to meet the weavin' geniuses and get to work.

I'd been outta use for some time. The Empress don't do much spinnin'—has her fancy frocks sent from Paris, France, she does. She'd never want to ding up them bony—I mean *delicate*—hands of hers, for sure.

But as soon as we're alone, the Weavers gave me the brush-off, titterin' on and on about the wool they was pullin' over the Emperor's eyes. Well, I'm a proper Spinnin' Wheel, I am! I don't cotton to them what spin yarns with lies and such. My spokes nearly bent out of shape, havin' to sit growin' cobwebs while them thievin' cheats thatched their plans.

Well, mark my words: The Wheel of Fortune spins slowly, but just like me giant wheel, what goes around, comes around. They'll get what's comin' to them, straight certain!

EANWHILE, the Emperor was eager to hear how things were moving along on his magnificent New Clothes. He sent his Imperial Dresser to visit the Weavers, commanding him to return with a progress report. The jittery man bustled by in such a rush, he created a breeze that sucked me along—

The Imperial Dresser

As told by Nathan Lane

ILLUSTRATED BY C. F. PAYNE

CLOTHES MAKE THE MAN; I pick the clothes. I don't like anyone interfering with my fashion turf, so when the Imperial Order came down for me to review the Weavers' work, I was eager to check out the competitors...and have them thrown out!

The Weavers began their presentation with lots of attitude, explaining that material of such a fine and rare nature could only be seen by visionaries gifted with true taste and imagination.

But when they pulled out the material, I (*gasp*) saw NOTHING! Was I losing my mind? Me, without taste? Impossible! I removed my spectacles and saw...BLURRIER NOTHING! Oh my.

The Emperor can be a bit fickle. He'd certainly fire a tasteless dresser! So I returned to my Imperial Employer and gushed: "Fabulous! Outragenifique! Oh, the...possibilities!"

Certainly, no one can say *I'm* not gifted with brilliant imagination!

The Dresser's Spectacles

As told by Jason Alexander

ILLUSTRATED BY MARK TEAGUE

IN ALL THE YEARS I've sat on the nose of the Imperial Dresser, no moment was more horrible than the instant he ripped me from his face and blamed his inability to see the Weavers' wares on my "tired lenses"!

All I long for is a soft case to hold me. A cloth to lie on. To be worn on a chain round the neck rather than crammed in a pocket. The simple things. Who needed this? With such savageness was I yanked off and tossed harshly onto the table, I'm surprised I didn't shatter from the force—and the humiliation.

The Weavers buzzed about the Dresser—*pant pant, fawn fawn*—showering him with attention, cutting patterns, prepping mannequins, and chiming, "Any suggestions? Your opinion means the *world* to us! Oh, do say you're pleased!" It was quite a wonderful bit of staging, but to the trained observer an obvious sham.

That nearsighted ninny fawning and cooing over those imaginary cloaks certainly made a fool of himself. What a spectacle indeed.

*T*HE DRESSER WAS SO UPSET by his experience with the Weavers, he went to see the pompous Imperial Physician to have his eyes examined and his nerves settled. I, of course, had to follow....

The Imperial Physician

As told by Dr. Ruth Westheimer

ILLUSTRATED BY STEVE JOHNSON & LOU FANCHER

ACH, THE PEOPLE in this Empire are *dummkopfs*. They whine of aches and pains, but they're as healthy as the oxen that pulled my father's plow back in Frankfurt. The Dresser is the worst, complaining of distorted vision. It's his brain that's distorted!

That fool pulled me from my important earwax research to examine the New Clothes. The Weavers spun around, raising dust clouds that made it difficult to see anything. But it was clear I was looking at NOTHING.

Then I discovered that the Emperor himself was eager to hear my fashion prognosis. I could care less about such matters, but the Emperor's blood pressure runs a little high, and the last thing I wanted to do was send it higher by criticizing his noble attire. My concern is his health, not his wardrobe! I went to his chambers and carefully injected my opinion: "Good choice, Herr Emperor! Such light and airy cloth will certainly not…irritate your sensitive Imperial Skin."

As for the Dresser's "faulty" spectacles, I came up with—uh, *recalled*—the Great Waldo Uberflaffer's Theory of Refractive Ocular Chimeraclarity: When seen through lenses, the Weavers' pattern bounces off the eye at 183 degrees, causing temporary blindness.

As I left the Emperor's chambers, I couldn't help but smile. Once again, I'd arrived at a brilliant diagnosis in a situation that would have left most physicians completely baffled!

JUST THEN THE EMPRESS caught wind of the New Clothes hubbub. She was overwhelmed with curiosity…and jealousy. With her Ladies-in-Waiting scurrying behind in her shadow, she marched off to the Weavers' salon to investigate.

The Empress

As told by Madonna

ILLUSTRATED BY DANIEL ADEL

"*Je suis l'Impératrice!*" For those who have been spared the rigors of intelligence, that's French for "I'm the Empress"—the better half of You-Know-Who.

Whatever I wear looks simply divine on me. When it comes to fashion influences, *I* do the influencing around here! It's exhausting, really. When I heard about *la pièce de résistance*, the Emperor's New Clothes, I had to give my approval. My husband—although loving and fair—isn't the sharpest knife in the drawer. I've got to watch out for him ... and me. *C'est la vie....*

I took one look at the Weavers' work and thought, *Where's the* joie de vivre, *the sequins, the* savoir faire? *It's just so* sans *everything. Is this a sick joke?* Then it dawned on me: In fashion it's important to make a statement. Have style. Take risks. Be bold. The Weavers had created a birthday suit simple in its elegance ... yet daring in its transparency!

If I wasn't so clever, I'd have missed it. *Quelle bonne idée!* I insisted they make one for *MOI* immediately.

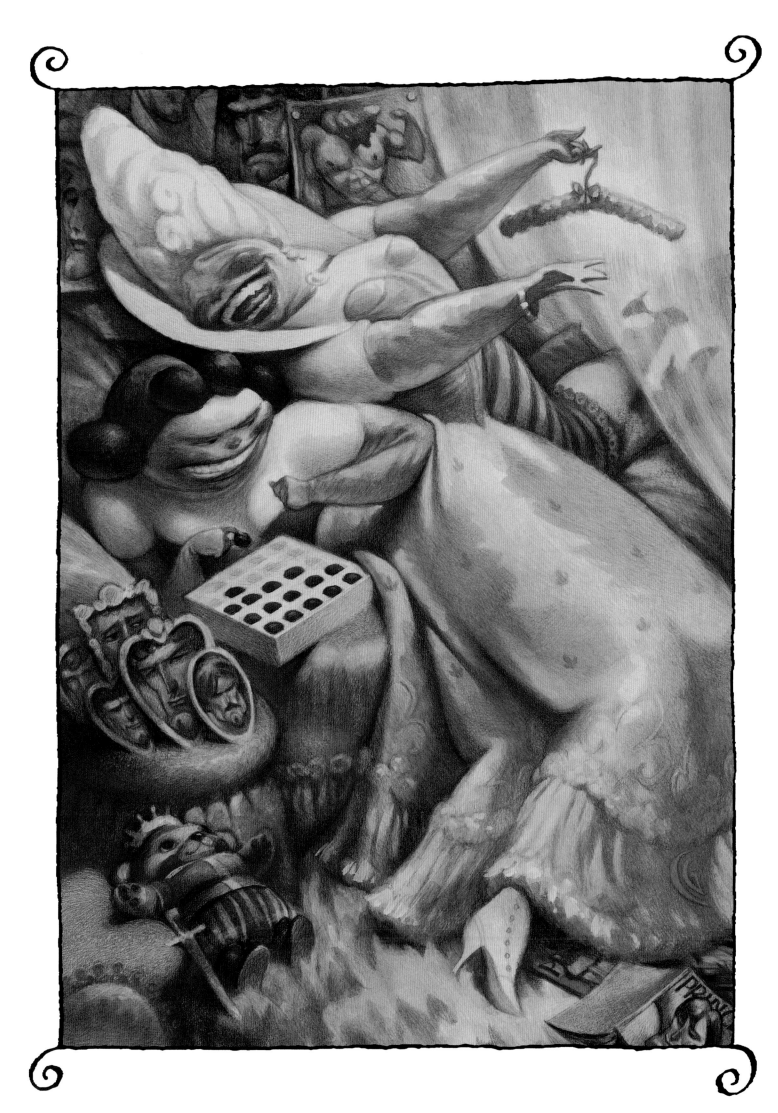

The Imperial Ladies-in-Waiting

As told by Carrie Fisher & Penny Marshall

ILLUSTRATED BY CARTER GOODRICH

I, BEATRINY VON BECKE, could have been—

No, I, Eugenia von Berg, *should* have been the Emperor's wife—
Instead we've been Ladies-in-Waiting since our early teens, when
Her Royal Bananahead married His Most Excellent Emperor. Now,
the closest we get to the good life is shadowing Wifey and indulging
her Empressy whims, like having to check out those Weavers.

Anyone could see those sniveling goombahs were thieves, but oh
no, not our little Imperial Nitwit. She ooh'd and ahh'd like a child
watching fireworks.

Until Eugenia had the gall to suggest the Noble Ninny get a *matching*
outfit to wear to the parade!

Bea laughed so hard, her head bobbed up and down. I think our
Birdbrain Boss thought Bea was nodding in agreement with my idea,
because at that exact moment, she commanded the Weavers to start
measuring *her* queenly carcass!

But it was completely the Royal Airhead's idea to have matching
outfits made for the children. It's a shame. Just because the mother's
a dingbat doesn't mean the kids should be made fools of, too.

So I respectfully said, "But, Empress, so many outfits of the same
material could belittle the dual splendor of you and the Emperor."
But Her Loopiness insisted. She sent for the children at once.

The Imperial Princess

As told by Melissa Joan Hart

ILLUSTRATED BY S. SAELIG GALLAGHER

AFTER MOM MADE US DRESS UP for visiting royalty to do a song-and-dance number from *The Sound of Music*, I swore: "Cassie, you'll never let that woman tell you what to wear again!" But Mom *is* still the Empress, and when she waves her hand and says, "Princess Cassandra must meet with the Imperial Weavers," you gotta go.

To tell the truth, the Weavers were not very well dressed, but I was taught to never judge a book by its cover. I mean, look at Albert Einstein: His hair was ridiculous, but the man was a genius.

They gave a big talk about stupid people not being able to see their cloth—*blah, blah, blah*—then showed me the New Clothes. I thought they were joking. They weren't.

There was no way I'd ever wear something so...revealing. So I made a deal with Mom: I'd wear one of those awful frilly princess rags she loves to see me in *if* I could pass on the Weavers' stuff. "The style is just too *simple* for me," I pleaded. "And so expensive! I'm afraid I'd ruin...such finery."

She went for it! Sure, I'd have to wear pink—but considering the alternative, I think I got the bargain end of the deal.

The Imperial Prince

As told by Jonathan Taylor Thomas

ILLUSTRATED BY GARY KELLEY

BEING PRINCE HAS ITS ADVANTAGES: money, servants, great food, an awesome palace to live in...but it's kind of a drag, too. Real kids aren't given names like Gunter Robert, and they are definitely not "sent for" by totally uncool empresses for fittings with Weavers.

I showed up with my Saint Bernard puppy, Small Fry. My first impression was that the Weavers needed weavers: Their "cloth" was invisible! *Totally cool,* I thought, *This should be in fashion for all the girls in the Empire!*

But then I realized I'd have to start the trend by wearing nothing at the parade myself. If my friends saw me, I'd be finished.

I got really nervous and started to babble. "I had a big lunch, I don't feel well, I'm late for an appointment, I have arthritis—er, bursitis, my dog needs to go for a walk, my dress shoes need shining, and...isn't it raining outside?"

The Weavers were speechless. Even Small Fry looked confused. I seized that moment to bolt to my conjuring lesson. Maybe the wizard could teach me how to disappear....

RACING OFF to see Tao, the Imperial Wizard, the Prince literally ran *bang* into his father. The Emperor, excited by the glowing reports he'd heard about his New Clothes, was anxious to know his boy's opinion of the Weavers' work.

The Prince stammered that he was late for his conjuring lesson but promised to get back to the Emperor in a flash. Then off we went to see the Wizard—befuddled boy, slobbering dog, and sneaky me.

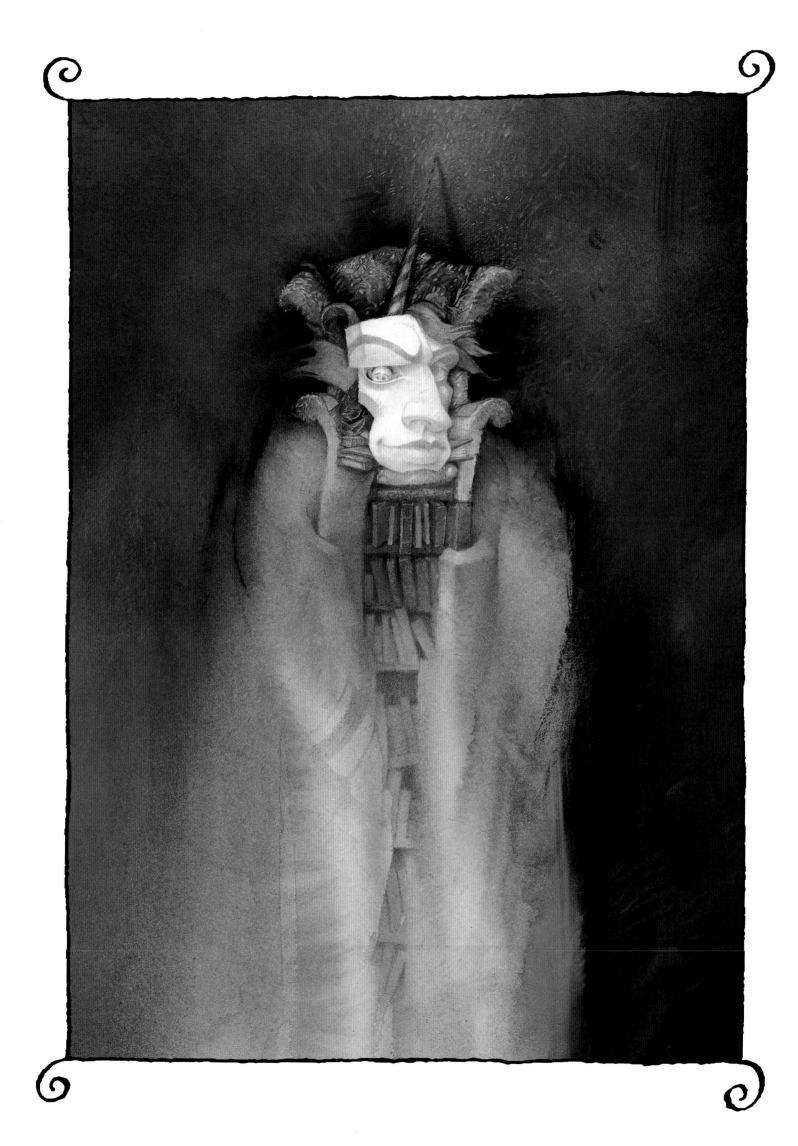

The Imperial Wizard

As told by Jeff Goldblum

ILLUSTRATED BY DAVID CHRISTIANA

THE PRINCE CAME TO ME experiencing confusion. He wanted to tell his father The Truth. "But how can I give an opinion of *nothing?*" the boy asked.

"The truth," I explained, "is like the blue of the sky—clouds may obscure it, but they'll eventually pass and the truth reemerges." He still seemed lost, so I tried another path: "Muddy waters can clear only when they are left alone. Leave this alone; so too will the truth settle." Yes, yes. The Doctrine of Inaction—one of my favorites, and always a safe bet.

The Prince seemed moved by my great insight. He asked me to view the cloth myself and to share my musings with the Emperor. I desire to leave no stone unturned—nor no boss's wish unheeded—and so I went. The Weavers had woven a cunning illusion, an impressive presentation that made everything quite clear.

I returned to the Emperor and bestowed upon him a gem of mystical wisdom: "The true sage may wear coarse garments, but he carries a jewel in his heart."

Ah yes. The Emperor was overjoyed, my student's confusion was eased, I had reeled off three perplexing proverbs—and all of this before lunch. Another day's work for a man in the know. Though I must admit that even I wasn't sure I knew what I meant!

$\mathcal{T}$AO'S SO DEEP, he's incomprehensible...which means no one ever understands a word he says. The Emperor is no exception: He just nodded and smiled at the old wizard's pronouncements...and sent for Etherius, the Imperial Holy Man.

Maybe a man of the cloth could bring the Emperor a little clarity....

The Holy Man

As told by Dan Aykroyd

ILLUSTRATED BY CHRIS VAN ALLSBURG

FASHION IS NOT CUSTOMARILY a religious concern, but my House of Worship—not to mention my fancy apartment, gourmet room service, generous personal allowance, and lavish carriage, with its team of white stallions—is all supported by the Emperor. So in all good faith, believe me when I say it was my…divine *pleasure* to oblige when he asked me to go bless his wondrous New Clothes.

The odd Weaver couple evangelically proclaimed that the clothes could be seen only by those possessing eternal intelligence and taste. Then they flourished, draped, and smoothed…THIN AIR. The pair finally dropped to their knees and asked me to bless the empty hanger from which their work "hung."

What could I do? I accept miracles every day. I prayed that this was one of them.

I returned to the Emperor and told him I found the fabric to be…*heavenly*.

How spiritually exhausting! The Emperor doesn't pay me enough for this.…

The Court Jester

As told by Robin Williams

ILLUSTRATED BY BERKELEY BREATHED

I'M THE BUTT of my jokes: My butt is the joke. I have a musical behind. A riotous rump. A talented *tuchus*. I entertain with my gift of gas. It's my special art.

I was performing my rendition of "Blowin' in the Wind" for the Emperor, when in burst the Holy Man, blowin' some wind of his own. I'd heard rumors about the New Clothes, but the Holy Windbag talked such a blue streak, I had to see them myself.

Well, when I got to the Weavers', I smelled something rotten...and for once it wasn't me! I overheard them cackling, "The old crow fool is almost ready! He can't wait to slip into his invisible birthday suit!"

I turned to butt out...and ran smack into His Royal Heinieness! He asked what I thought of his New Clothes. As my father, Harry B. Hind, always said: "Know which side your butt is bettered on"—I was not going to lie, or deliver bad news.

I said, "Very revealing, Your Grace. They'll undoubtedly show off your assets!" Then I made a hasty exit and broke like the wind!

THE WEAVERS finally sent word that they were ready for a fitting. The Emperor summoned all of his advisors to his Imperial Dressing Room for the big moment.

The Weavers carefully "fitted" the New Clothes on the Emperor. They fussed and tugged on this and that, then finally stood back, nodding approvals and gushing compliments.

The Prime Minister watched it all with a creepy smile…then humbly suggested that the Emperor should turn around and look in the Imperial Mirror to at last see the New Clothes for himself.

The Imperial Mirror

As told by Geena Davis

ILLUSTRATED BY KINUKO Y. CRAFT

I'M PERFECT.

No, really—I am. Faultless. Impeccable. Unclouded. Quite simply, *incapable* of making a mistake. I reflect things exactly as they are. And *nothing* gets by me.

Sure, the Emperor and I have haggled about the size of his bald spot over the years, but he always ends up seeing things my way. Which is exactly why I'd watched the Weavers' theatrics with such amusement. I was certain that once the Emperor took a good look into my glass at the Great Final Fitting, he would see the truth and, together, we'd shatter the thieves' scam. Picture this: MIRROR SAVES THE DAY.

Well, the Emperor stepped in front of me and we gazed at each other. His eyes searched the reflection but kept darting to his advisors behind him. *Surely* he saw what I unmistakably mirrored: a framed, nearly naked Emperor; a twitchy pair of "weavers"; the sinister Prime Minister; and the whole nodding Imperial Court of Fools.

But the Emperor didn't say a word! No one said anything! I just about cracked in frustration. I thought the Emperor was a sensible man. I was showing him everything, clear as could be. My gilded glory! What was he possibly thinking?

THE SILENCE WAS BROKEN by a cry of great joy…which none of the *people* were able to hear. It came from the most unlikely of places.

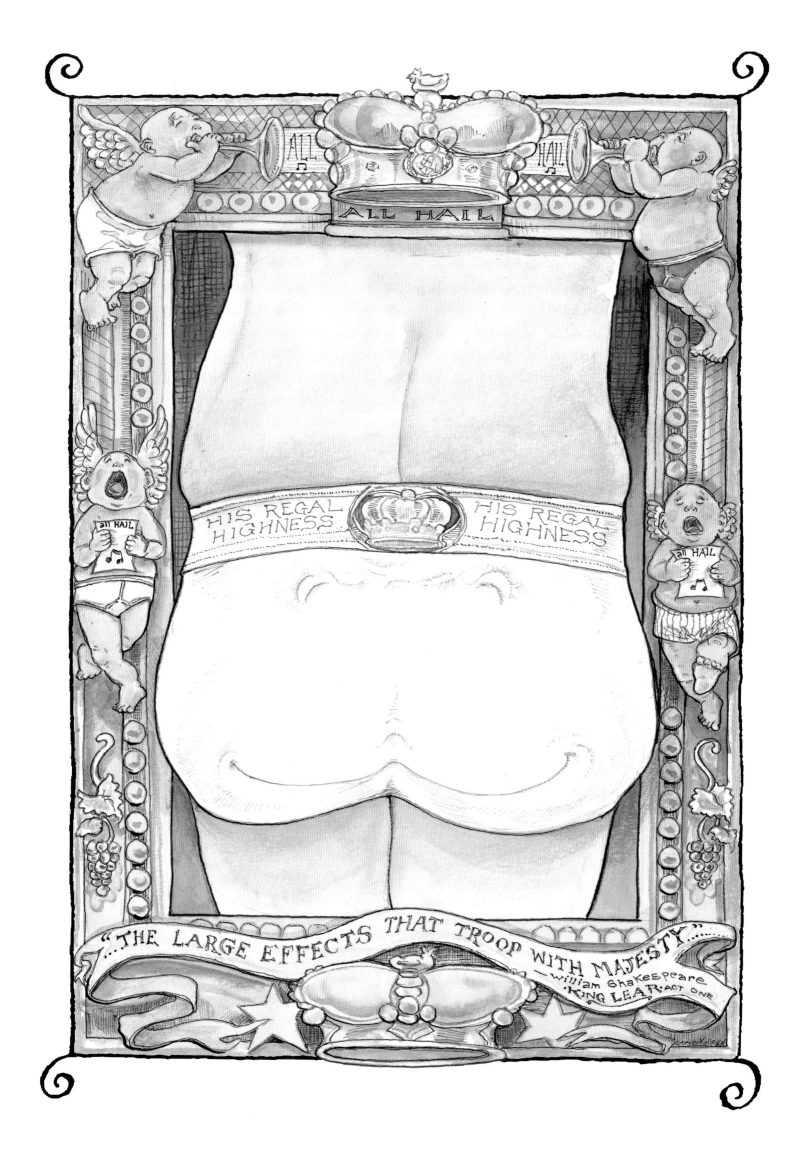

The Emperor's Underwear

As told by Calvin Klein

ILLUSTRATED BY STEVEN KELLOGG

"Yippeee!" I was so pleased to see myself—looking especially smart and trim—in the Imperial Mirror.

Of everyone in the Imperial Dressing Room, no one was more purely and sincerely excited about the Emperor's forthcoming birthday parade than I was. I've always gone along with and been close to the Emperor, but his wise decision to go with these New Clothes was one I was especially happy to fully support. I'd had enough of undercover work; my lifelong dream was to be seen in public. At the parade, I would finally be the star!

I simply could not wait to hear the crowd's cheers. Nothing comes between me and my Emperor!

The Imperial Throne

As told by Rosie O'Donnell

ILLUSTRATED BY TOMIE DEPAOLA

I KNOW THIS is hard to believe, but—off the record—the Emperor doesn't always wear the finest underwear. Lord knows he can afford the good stuff. I often wonder if his mother brought him up correctly. Sometimes his undies look like Swiss cheese.

I just wish I could tell His Imperialness about that manipulating, conniving Prime Minister. Whence—right or wrong, I say *whence*—all the kingdom is asleep, he quietly tiptoes into the Emperor's chambers, plants his bottom on me, and pretends to be the boss! With dirty feet, no less! And just for the record: The Prime Minister's behind is rough and coarse, and has more hair on it than the Princess's pet orangutan.

Anyhow, when I saw the Emperor coming toward me to sit down, I was not prepared for his...bare essentials, shall we say. Four legs I've got, and yet I couldn't run away. The Emperor is a kind, decent, benevolent man, and his behind is softer than silk, more tender than a thousand babies' bottoms. But c'mon: I prefer my royal heinies *unexposed*!

$\mathcal{T}$HE EMPEROR STOOD UP from his throne and announced: "These are the *finest* threads I think I've ever seen!"

Just then the Weaver lady cleared her throat and started making funny eyes at her husband. "Forgive my *husband*, Yer Majesty, but he nearly forgot one of the most important pieces of the ensemble," she said, jamming her elbow into the Weaver man's ribs. "The Imperial *Undergarment*."

"Oh yeah," her husband said, stumbling forward. "Got it right here." He bowed his head and acted like he was holding something delicate in his bony fingers. "Behold your extra-special birthday briefs. Our very special gift. No charge."

The Emperor thanked the Weavers and gingerly accepted his "underwear." He solemnly promised to wear them on the big day.

The Prime Minister beamed.

The wails and sobs that came screeching out of the "old" Imperial Underwear were so loud, I couldn't believe no one heard them. I've never seen a more disappointed piece of cotton in my life.

And then the Emperor's Birthday arrived.

The heralding horn

As told by Fran Drescher

ILLUSTRATED BY MICHAEL PARASKEVAS

THEY CALL ME the Hedda Hopper of horns—I get the word out. Sometimes all the *geshreien* (yelling) wears on my pipes, but my voice is insured by Lloyd's of London. One day I'll be a very quiet but rich horn. . . .

Anyway, the sun was shining, kids were playing, birds were singing, everyone in the fancy-schmancy procession was lining up, ready to go. . . . And in the middle of it all stood two Imperial Pink Blobs—the most gullible schmucks I'd ever seen. I couldn't believe the Emperor and his wife were buying into this *meshuggaas*!

But it was time for me to trumpet the royal fanfare . . . and for the people to wonder where their tax money was going with these morons at the helm.

My full, brassy lips carried my tune to the streets, but I was really blasting: "Hear ye, hear ye! Today will live in infamy! Trust me, you ain't seen nothing yet! *Oy vey.*"

THE HERALDING HORN could barely be heard over the din of the excited crowd. As the parade began, everyone pushed forward to get a glimpse of the Emperor's New Clothes.

Of course, for me the crowd was a smorgasbord waiting to happen. I spotted an overdressed woman on the sidelines and made a beeline for her shawl...which I nibbled like movie popcorn as I watched the big show.

The Honest Boy's Mother

As told by Joan Rivers

ILLUSTRATED BY FRED MARCELLINO

I GUESS THE EMPEROR blew the parade budget on his New Clothes. We expected ballerinas, jugglers, and dancing bears, but all we got were a couple of three-hundred-pound ballerinas who couldn't plié and a juggler "juggling" one ball, which he dropped. Next came the Emperor's dogs, followed by the Empress's sisters—two groups easily confused.

Finally, bringing up the rear, there were two unattractive naked people to whom aerobics was clearly a foreign concept.

Ugh, I thought, *even a crown can't distract from ugly cellulite*. Yes, the fact that the royal couple were naked crossed my mind, but so did visions of being in a prison tower and having my head lopped off for speaking out against the Emperor.

My son started pestering me, pulling on my skirt and trying to be heard over the crummy sixty-seven-tuba band. He finally kicked me, which no son should do to such a young and attractive mother. "The Emperor and the Empress have no clothes," he whispered.

"Shut up, already," I said, trying to protect him. "The clothes are flesh colored—can't you see the pretty blue lines in the Empress's stockings?"

The Honest Boy

As told by Steven Spielberg

ILLUSTRATED BY DON WOOD

WAS MY MOM losing her mind? Was *everyone* whacko? Or was I the nut case? I *knew* what I was seeing....I mean, I was 99.9999 percent sure I knew what I was seeing. But people were acting weird, saying, "I love it!" "The outfit is so... uncomplicated!" And "They've outdone themselves this time!"

HUH? I pushed through the jungle of grown-ups' legs and got my toes right on the edge of the line where a sign read: PLEASE DO NOT CROSS. And then I leaned *wa-aa-ay* forward and squinted *really* hard....

"*THE EMPEROR AND EMPRESS ARE NAKED!!!*"

Finally! Somebody had told The Truth!

Ooops. That *somebody* was ME.

I hadn't realized how loud I was until I heard "*NAKED-ED-ED-ED-ED*" echoing off the castle walls. My mom tried to cover my mouth but ended up just sticking her finger up my nose. Everyone shut up at the exact same second, and the whole parade *stopped* right in front of me. Thousands of people were staring. My heart started pounding so hard, I thought my ribs were gonna crack; the rumbling in my ears got louder and louder.

Was I completely busted? Or was I just...*right?*

*T*HE RUMBLING THE BOY HEARD was coming not from inside of his head but from the crowd: "He's right . . . the boy's *right!*" they were saying. The rumbling grew into a ruckus. Things were looking bad for the Royal Family and the entire humiliated Imperial Court. The people of the Empire were about to riot!

Just then the Imperial General—an imposing man who thought quickly on his feet—sprang into action.

The Imperial General

As told by Gen. H. Norman Schwarzkopf

ILLUSTRATED BY GRAEME BASE

IN ALL THE CONFUSION, I spied an evil grin creeping across the Prime Minister's face. I knew he was up to no good. I'd been certain for some time that he was lining his pockets with the People's money, waiting for a chance to overthrow the Emperor. But the Prime Minister wasn't going to get his chance. Not on my watch.

I positioned myself close to the Emperor and quietly *congratulated* him on his successful plan to uncover evil influences in the government. He had no idea what I was talking about . . . until I helped him "realize" that the parade was a plan—*his* plan—to turn the tables on the Prime Minister and the Weavers, to expose their dastardly plot by exposing *himself*!

That little weasel of a prime minister was shaking all over when I grabbed him. He knew his plan had failed . . . and that with just a slight bit more pressure, I could snap his wicked neck!

The sniffling plotters begged for mercy as I carted them off. The Prime Minister blamed the Weavers and the Weavers, of course, blamed him right back. Spineless scoundrels.

My duty was done. The stage was set for the Emperor to speak.

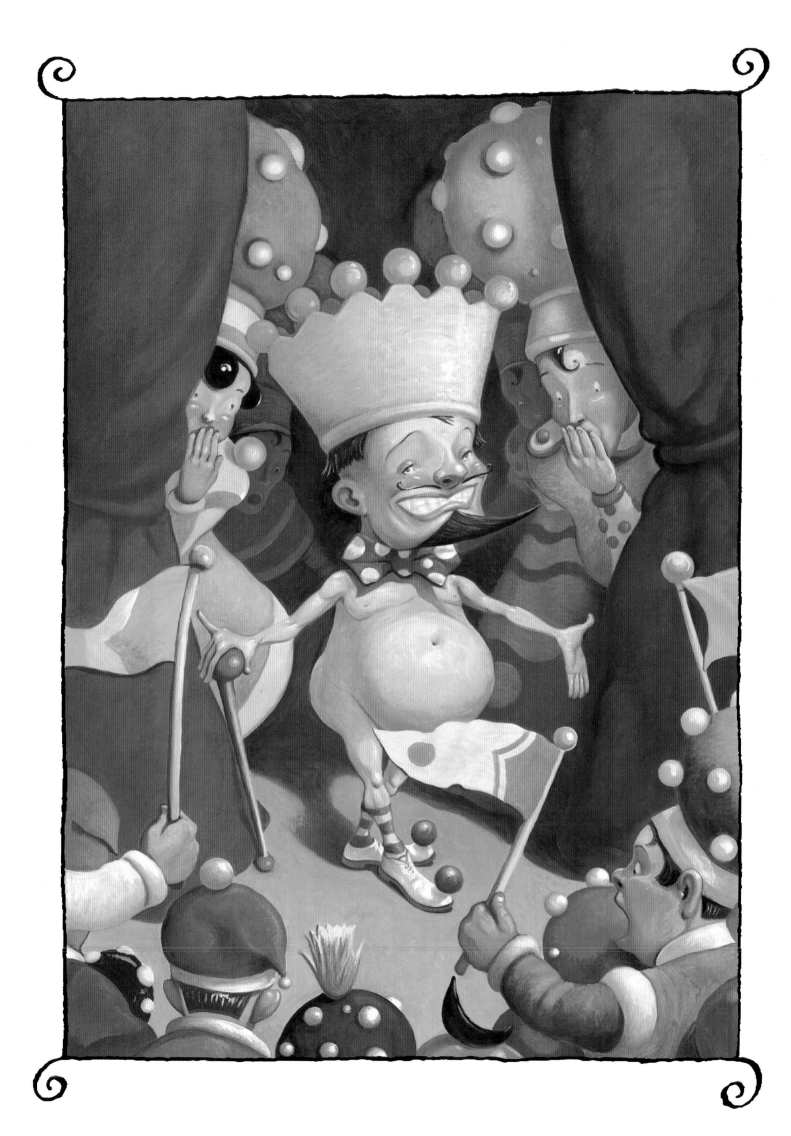

The Emperor

As told by John Lithgow

ILLUSTRATED BY WILLIAM JOYCE

"CITIZENS!

Your Emperor, Trent Trendycrest, demands your attention!

The ousted Prime Minister has just lost his pension.

You see, this parade was a clever charade

To expose two impostors and one renegade.

"Today is a day for great celebration!

We are rid of those villains; peace and joy fill our nation.

But now I am faced with a vacant high post—

A trusted advisor is what I need most.

"I have someone in mind who is brave, smart, and true,

Not to mention his tunic's a nice shade of blue....

So, my people, the residents of this fine land,

I present our new Prime Minister—the Honest Boy! Let's give him a hand!"

I then asked the boy how he'd honestly feel

If I wore brown suede shoes with a black belt of eel.

Without missing a beat, he planted his feet,

And spoke loudly and clearly to the whole crowded street:

"It just doesn't matter if your clothes are tattered,
Or woven from fine golden thread.
It's what's in your heart that makes you look smart,
Not to mention the *brain* in your head."

The crowd cheered, and a wide path was cleared,
And when the boy raised his medal, his mother's eyes teared.
And perhaps even I had a tear in my eye—
An emotion the greatest of wealth couldn't buy.

Yes, honesty's always the best policy:
Tell the whole naked truth when you see what you see.
But I'd never have learned that, I surely suppose,
If I hadn't been wearing the Emperor's New Clothes.

AND, YOU GUESSED IT,

$\mathcal{E}$VERYONE LIVED HAPPILY EVER AFTER.

Everyone, that is, except the former Prime Minister and the Weavers.

To this day the evil trio is on public display in a big glass box in front of the palace. All day and all night, they weave and sew new clothes (real ones) to be given away to everyone in the Empire. And—although some say this is more of a punishment for the townspeople—the three are forced to do their work naked!

They're awful tailors; they make a lot of mistakes. But thanks to them, I'm a very happy moth. My belly stays full from the tasty scraps that pile high behind the glass box.

In the meantime, do a friendly moth a favor: Tell your parents to get rid of those mothballs and cedar chips, and who knows? Maybe I'll wing by for a visit....

The Cast

IN ORDER OF APPEARANCE

THE MOTH

QUENTIN BLAKE is the internationally acclaimed illustrator of more than two hundred award-winning children's books, among them *Mister Magnolia*, for which he was awarded the Kate Greenaway Medal, and *Mrs. Armitage and the Big Wave*. He is especially adored by young readers as the illustrator of a number of Roald Dahl novels, including *The BFG*, *The Twits*, *The Witches*, and *Matilda*.

THE IMPERIAL PRIME MINISTER

LIAM NEESON began his career on the Irish stage. Director John Boorman saw him in an Abbey Theatre production of *Of Mice and Men* and cast him in the Arthurian epic *Excalibur*. He has continued to work in both theater and movies, and has appeared in some thirty films, including *The Mission*, *Suspect*, *Husbands and Wives*, *Rob Roy*, *Michael Collins*, *Les Miserables*, and the *Star Wars* prequel.

THE IMPERIAL PRIME MINISTER

MAURICE SENDAK is the creator of the beloved classic *Where the Wild Things Are*, for which he received the Caldecott Medal in 1964. He has written and illustrated dozens of other books, won many of the major awards for children's literature, designed operas and created television shows, and—over the course of more than four decades— has challenged established ideas about what children's literature is and should be. His many popular books include *In the Night Kitchen*, *Outside Over There*, and *We Are All in the Dumps with Jack and Guy*.

THE WEAVER THIEVES

HARRISON FORD & MELISSA MATHISON have been married for fifteen years. He is an actor, she is a screenwriter. They live in Jackson Hole, Wyoming, with their two young children. They neither weave nor steal.

THE WEAVER THIEVES

PETER de SÈVE's artwork is familiar to Broadway playgoers for his posters for both *Candide* and *A Funny Thing Happened on the Way to the Forum*. A frequent contributor of covers to national magazines such as *The New Yorker*, he also works for Hollywood animation studios. He has helped develop characters for Disney features including *The Hunchback of Notre Dame*, and for the DreamWorks SKG film *The Prince of Egypt*.

THE SPINNING WHEEL

ANGELA LANSBURY's career spans more than half a century. She has enjoyed enormous success as a motion picture actress, as a star of dramatic and musical theater on Broadway, and as the heroine of *Murder, She Wrote*, one of the longest running detective dramas in the history of television. She was also the voice of Mrs. Potts in Disney's *Beauty and the Beast*. Her work has won her numerous awards and honors, including six Golden Globes and four Tony Awards.

THE SPINNING WHEEL

ETIENNE DELESSERT's critically acclaimed books began delighting children and parents in 1967, with the publication of his *The Endless Party*. He has since illustrated more than fifty books, including *A Long Long Song* and *Dance!* In addition to creating children's books, he also contributes illustrations to national magazines. Delessert's work was recognized early by a worldwide audience; the first retrospective of his art was held at the Louvre when he was just thirty-four.

THE IMPERIAL DRESSER

NATHAN LANE is a favorite of stage and screen audiences for the comic energy he brings to his roles. His performance in the hit movie *The Birdcage*, in which he played opposite Robin Williams, earned him an American Comedy Award, a Screen Actors Guild Award, and a Golden Globe nomination. For his performance in the hugely successful Broadway revival of *A Funny Thing Happened on the Way to the Forum*, he was awarded Tony, Drama Desk, and Outer Critics Circle Awards.

THE IMPERIAL DRESSER

C. F. PAYNE is a freelance illustrator whose work frequently appears in *Time*, *The New York Times Book Review*, *Esquire*, *GQ*, and *The New Yorker*, among many other national magazines. He has taught and lectured extensively, and his many honors include gold and silver medals and the Hamilton King Award from the Society of Illustrators. In the fall of 1996, his work was recognized with an exhibition at the Cincinnati Art Museum.

THE DRESSER'S SPECTACLES

JASON ALEXANDER is best known to television audiences as hapless schlemiel George Costanza on *Seinfeld*, but his acting career spans more than twenty years of stage, screen, and television. He has played supporting roles in *Pretty Woman*, *The Paper*, and many other films, and he starred in *Love! Valour! Compassion!* He also voiced the characters of Hugo the gargoyle in Disney's *The Hunchback of Notre Dame* and the title role of the adult cartoon *Duckman*.

THE DRESSER'S SPECTACLES

MARK TEAGUE's first children's book, *The Trouble with the John-sons*, inspired *Publishers Weekly* to name him one of eleven prominent new artists and writers of 1989. Never formally trained as a writer or illustrator, he has defined his appealingly weird style in a dozen notable books, including his own *Baby Tamer*, *Pigsty*, and *The Secret Shortcut*, and as the illustrator of *The Flying Dragon Room* by Audrey Wood and the series of books about Poppleton the pig by Cynthia Rylant.

THE IMPERIAL PHYSICIAN

DR. RUTH WESTHEIMER is the psychosexual therapist Americans turn to when they have questions about sex. Her groundbreaking radio program *Sexually Speaking* introduced Dr. Ruth to audiences in 1980, and since then she has brought her expertise to millions through nearly every media, including weekly newspaper columns, books, games, home videos, computer software, the Internet, and the internationally syndicated television show *Ask Dr. Ruth*.

THE IMPERIAL PHYSICIAN

STEVE JOHNSON & LOU FANCHER are a husband-and-wife team and the illustrators of many highly acclaimed books for children, including Dr. Seuss's *My Many Colored Days*, Garrison Keillor's *Cat, You Better Come Home*, and Jon Scieszka's *The Frog Prince, Continued*. Longtime admirers of late ballerina Dame Margot Fonteyn, the pair recently created illustrations for Fonteyn's retelling of *Coppélia*. They live in Minneapolis, Minnesota.

THE EMPRESS

MADONNA burst onto the music scene in 1982 with her self-titled debut album, which began a string of hit records that continues to this day—and that has made her one of the most popular singers around the world. She has also become one of Hollywood's favorite leading ladies, starring in films including *Desperately Seeking Susan*, *Dick Tracy*, *A League of Their Own*, and the film version of the Andrew Lloyd Weber musical *Evita*, in which she played the title role.

THE EMPRESS

DANIEL ADEL has been working as a freelance illustrator since graduating from Dartmouth College in 1984. He has painted numerous portraits, illustrated the children's book *The Book That Jack Wrote* by Jon Scieszka, and has created illustrations for the covers and pages of many national magazines, including *Vanity Fair*, *The New Yorker*, and *Time*. In his spare time, Mr. Adel practices neurosurgery.

THE IMPERIAL LADIES-IN-WAITING

CARRIE FISHER is an accomplished actress, best-selling novelist, and highly regarded screenwriter. Catapulted to fame by her leading role as Princess Leia in the blockbuster *Star Wars* trilogy, she has appeared in many other films, including *When Harry Met Sally* and *Hannah and Her Sisters*. She later turned her talents to the page and wrote the best-selling *Postcards from the Edge*, two other novels, and a number of screenplays.

PENNY MARSHALL and Cindy Williams made up the beloved duo of *Laverne & Shirley*, one of the most successful comedy series in television history. After the show's seven-year run, she moved behind the cameras and distinguished herself as the director of many notable films. *Big*, her second movie, won Tom Hanks his first Oscar nomination for best actor; her film *A League of Their Own* was a box-office success; and *Awakenings* was nominated for an Academy Award for best picture.

THE IMPERIAL LADIES-IN-WAITING

CARTER GOODRICH regularly creates artwork for national magazines such as *Time*, *Forbes*, *GQ*, and *The New Yorker*, and has also illustrated two classics for children, *The Nutcracker* and *A Christmas Carol*. He has also worked on animated character development for Fox, Pixar, and DreamWorks SKG, for which he was a chief stylist for the feature-length animated film *The Prince of Egypt*.

THE IMPERIAL PRINCESS

MELISSA JOAN HART shot her first national commercial when she was just four years old, and she's been working nonstop ever since. She has acted in commercials and television shows, appeared on Broadway in *The Crucible*, and wrote a popular advice column for the teen magazine *Teen Beat*. Her two most well-known roles thus far in her career have been Clarissa on Nickelodeon's *Clarissa Explains It All* and the title role of *Sabrina, the Teenage Witch*.

THE IMPERIAL PRINCESS

S. SAELIG GALLAGHER's paintings have been featured in books for both adults and children, and have been published in newspapers and magazines throughout the country. Her work has received many awards and honors, including a silver medal from the Society of Illustrators. Her first picture book, *Moonhorse* by Mary Pope Osborne, was highly praised, and her subsequent books—including *The Selfish Giant* by Oscar Wilde—have brought her increasingly wide recognition as a distinguished children's book illustrator.

THE IMPERIAL PRINCE

JONATHAN TAYLOR THOMAS plays Randy, the middle son, on the popular television series *Home Improvement*. He has also acted in several notable motion pictures, including *Wild America*, *Tom and Huck*, *Man of the House*, and *The Adventures of Pinnochio*. He contributes voice-overs for many animated characters, most notably the voice of Young Simba in Disney's *The Lion King*.

THE IMPERIAL PRINCE

GARY KELLEY has created artwork for magazine covers, record jackets, and major advertising campaigns, as well as picture books. His illustrated classics include Washington Irving's *The Legend of Sleepy Hollow* and *Rip Van Winkle*, Guy de Maupassant's *The Necklace*, and Edgar Allan Poe's *Tales of Mystery and Imagination*. He has received many awards, including twenty-three medals from the Society of Illustrators as well as its Hamilton King Award for achievement in illustration.

THE IMPERIAL WIZARD

JEFF GOLDBLUM began his career at age seventeen, when he moved to New York to study acting at the Neighborhood Playhouse. Within a few years, Goldblum had landed his first parts in *Death Wish* and *Nashville*. He has since become well recognized for his roles in films such as *The Big Chill*, *Silverado*, *The Fly*, *Jurassic Park*, *The Lost World*, and *Independence Day*. A short film he directed, *Little Surprises*, was nominated for an Academy Award.

THE IMPERIAL WIZARD

DAVID CHRISTIANA made his solo debut as a children's book writer and illustrator with his acclaimed *Drawer in a Drawer* in 1990. He has since been recognized as one of the brightest talents in children's book illustration, both for his work on his own books, including *White Nineteens*, and for his illustrations for books written by other heralded authors, including *Good Griselle* by Jane Yolen and *I Am the Mummy Heb-Nefert* by Eve Bunting.

THE HOLY MAN

DAN AYKROYD got his start with Toronto's famed Second City comedy troupe, but it was for his work with the original *Saturday Night Live* lineup in 1975 that he first came to prominence. After leaving *SNL*, he acted in a number of comic films, including *Ghostbusters*, *Dragnet*, and *Grosse Pointe Blank*. Though primarily known as a comedian, he has also been honored for his dramatic work—including an Academy Award nomination for best supporting actor for *Driving Miss Daisy*.

THE HOLY MAN

CHRIS VAN ALLSBURG is one of the most popular creators of children's books in the United States. His Caldecott Medal–winning *The Polar Express* is a Christmas classic, and his book *Jumanji*, another Caldecott Medal winner, was made into a hit movie starring Robin Williams. His other books include *The Garden of Abdul Gasazi*, a Caldecott Honor Book; *The Widow's Broom*; *Two Bad Ants*; and three storybooks by Mark Helprin, including *Swan Lake* and *A City in Winter*.

THE COURT JESTER

ROBIN WILLIAMS rocketed into the public eye in the 1970s as the hyperactive alien Mork from Ork, first on *Happy Days* and then on the spin-off *Mork and Mindy*. One of the most gifted actors in Hollywood, he has acted in both comic and dramatic films, including *The World According to Garp*, *Dead Poets Society*, *The Fisher King*, *Mrs. Doubtfire*, *Flubber*, and—as the voice of the wisecracking genie—Disney's hit *Aladdin*. He has been nominated for the Academy Award three times, and has won four Grammy Awards.

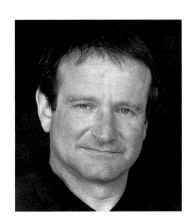

THE COURT JESTER

BERKELEY BREATHED is a cartoonist, author of children's books, and screenwriter. His Pulitzer Prize–winning comic strip, *Bloom County* (1980–89), was one of the most popular strips of the eighties. His first picture book, *A Wish for Wings That Work*, featured one of his most popular *Bloom County* characters, the penguin Opus, and was made into a half-hour animated television special. He is also the author of *The Last Basselope*, *Red Ranger Came Calling*, and many other books.

THE IMPERIAL MIRROR

GEENA DAVIS made her film debut in *Tootsie* in 1982. Since then she has become one of Hollywood's most popular actresses, garnering an Academy Award nomination for her performance in *Thelma & Louise* and winning an Oscar for best supporting actress for *The Accidental Tourist*. Her other films include *Beetlejuice*, *A League of Their Own*, and *The Long Kiss Goodnight*.

THE IMPERIAL MIRROR

KINUKO Y. CRAFT's paintings frequently appear on the covers of national magazines such as *Time* and *Newsweek*, and she has created illustrations for the covers of dozens of novels. She has won more than one hundred graphic arts awards, including three gold medals from the Society of Illustrators. Her children's books include *Cupid and Psyche* (as told by M. Charlotte Craft), *The Twelve Dancing Princesses*, and *Baba Yaga and Vasilisa the Brave* (both as told by Mariana Mayer).

THE EMPEROR'S UNDERWEAR

CALVIN KLEIN's name ranks among the best-known brand names in the world, a fitting tribute to a driven boy from the Bronx who dreamed of becoming a designer—and who taught himself to sketch and sew. He is well known not only for his clothing lines, which encompass everything from regal underwear to designer jeans to high fashion men's and women's wear, but also for his pioneering advertising campaigns, his popular fragrances, and his philanthropic efforts on behalf of several AIDS foundations.

THE EMPEROR'S UNDERWEAR

STEVEN KELLOGG has drawn pictures for most of his life—as a kid, he amused his sisters by illustrating stories he made up. As an adult, he has illustrated dozens of books, thirty of which he also wrote. His books include the popular stories about Pinkerton the Great Dane, James Thurber's *The Great Quillow*, and a retelling of *Jack and the Beanstalk*, which was named an ALA Notable Book. His many awards include the Regina Medal, which honors artists for distinguished contributions to children's literature.

ROSIE O'DONNELL is considered one of Hollywood's top comedic actresses for her roles in *A League of Their Own*, *Sleepless in Seattle*, *The Flintstones*, and *Beautiful Girls*. She has become a favorite of television critics and audiences alike for her hugely successful talk show, *The Rosie O'Donnell Show*. Named "Entertainer of the Year" by *Entertainment Weekly*, she has been praised for bringing a welcome warmth and humor to the talk show circuit.

TOMIE dePAOLA is an enormously popular children's book illustrator whose simple, stylized artwork is instantly recognizable. The creator of nearly one hundred books since his first in 1965—and the illustrator of many more—he has won a Caldecott Honor for *Strega Nona*, a Kerlan Award, and the Regina Medal, as well as many other honors. Among his most popular books are *Strega Nona* and its sequels, *The Clown of God*, and *Tomie dePaola's Mother Goose*.

FRAN DRESCHER, the brassy-voiced star of television's *The Nanny*, got her start on the big screen, appearing in *Saturday Night Fever*, *This Is Spinal Tap*, *Ragtime*, and many other movies. Her film credits also include *The Beautician and the Beast* and *Jack*, in which she played Robin Williams's love interest. A two-time Emmy nominee, she has also shown a talent for writing: Her autobiography, *Enter Whining*, was a national best-seller.

MICHAEL PARASKEVAS and his mother, Betty Paraskevas, form one of the most original creative teams in children's books. Their four books about the irrepressible Junior Kroll are cult classics, and their other books, including *The Ferocious Beast*, *Cecil Bunions and the Midnight Train*, and *The Tangerine Bear*, are beloved by readers and critics alike. Michael Paraskevas also produces artwork for magazines such as *Sports Illustrated* and *Time*, and regularly exhibits in galleries.

THE HONEST BOY'S MOTHER

JOAN RIVERS is a comedienne, author, actress, playwright, business woman, and mother, but is perhaps best known for her Emmy Award–winning talk show. The first sole permanent guest hostess of *The Tonight Show*, she has since gone on to host E! Entertainment Television's "Fashion Reviews" and, with her daughter, Melissa, E!'s preshow commentary for the Emmy, Golden Globe, and Academy Award telecasts. She has written six books and can be heard nightly on the WOR radio network.

THE HONEST BOY'S MOTHER

FRED MARCELLINO was born and lives in New York City. Before he began illustrating children's books, he was already well regarded for his distinctive book jackets. His first picture book, *Puss in Boots*, was published to great acclaim in 1990 and was named a Caldecott Honor Book. His other books include *The Steadfast Tin Soldier*, *The Pelican Chorus and Other Nonsense*, and *The Story of Little Babaji*.

THE HONEST BOY

STEVEN SPIELBERG is one of the world's most respected filmmakers. He made his first film with actors at the age of twelve, and has since directed many of the most successful films in the history of motion pictures, including *Jaws*, *E.T.*, *Close Encounters of the Third Kind*, *Raiders of the Lost Ark*, and both *Jurassic Park* films, as well as many acclaimed dramas, among them *The Color Purple* and *Amistad*. He won Academy Awards for best picture and best director for *Schindler's List*.

THE HONEST BOY

DON WOOD is a Caldecott Honor illustrator for his work on *King Bidgood's in the Bathtub*. He and his wife, author Audrey Wood, are one of the most successful children's book illustrating-and-writing teams of the past twenty years. Their book *The Napping House*, a *New York Times* Best Illustrated Book, is a perennial favorite, as are their other collaborations: *Heckedy Peg*, *Piggies*, *The Tickleoctopus*, and *Bright and Early Thursday Evening*, among others.

THE IMPERIAL GENERAL

GEN. H. NORMAN SCHWARZKOPF, U.S. Army, Retired, served as Commander in Chief of Operations Desert Shield and Desert Storm. He coordinated the efforts of all allied forces from August 1990, soon after Iraq invaded Kuwait, until August 1991, when he retired. He has written a best-selling autobiography, *It Doesn't Take a Hero*, appeared in several television specials, and devotes much of his time to philanthropic efforts, including The Nature Conservancy and the STARBRIGHT Capital Campaign.

THE IMPERIAL GENERAL

GRAEME BASE's career began auspiciously: He was fired from his first post-collegiate job for incompetence. He turned to illustration and has never looked back. His picture book *Animalia*, an alliterative alphabet book, was a best-seller around the world. Like his other books, *Animalia* features engagingly complicated illustrations that appeal to both children and adults. He has also published *The Eleventh Hour*, *The Sign of the Seahorse*, and *The Discovery of Dragons*.

THE EMPEROR

JOHN LITHGOW is familiar to television audiences for his out-of-this-world portrayal of an alien in the comedy series *3rd Rock from the Sun*, but he has been been a mainstay of theater, film, and television for many years. He won a Tony for his Broadway debut in *The Changing Room*, earned Academy Award nominations for his performances in *The World According to Garp* and *Terms of Endearment*, and has been honored with two Emmy Awards and a Golden Globe for his continuing role on *3rd Rock from the Sun*.

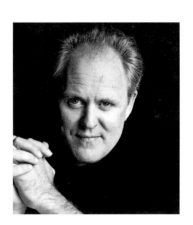

THE EMPEROR

WILLIAM JOYCE has become one of the preeminent illustrators of children's books since his first book appeared in the mid-1980s. His stylized illustrations recall an America that never was—a world and era all Joyce's own. His paintings appear on the covers of national magazines such as *The New Yorker*, and his many books include *Santa Calls*, *A Day with Wilbur Robinson*, *Dinosaur Bob*, and *The Leaf Men*.

The text type was set in Jensen.

The display type was set in Goudy Mediaeval.

Hand lettering and borders by Georgia Deaver

Color separations by Bright Arts, Ltd., Hong Kong

Printed and bound by RRDonnelley & Sons, Reynosa, Mexico

This book was printed on totally chlorine-free Nymolla Matte Art paper.

Production supervision by Stanley Redfern

Art direction and design by Michael Farmer

Many of the images featured in this book are available as limited edition art prints, exclusively from

Storyopolis Productions, 116 North Robertson Boulevard, Plaza Level Suite A, Los Angeles, California 90048; (310) 358-2525.

The Emperor's New Clothes

COMPACT DISC CREDITS

The Imperial Prime Minister written and performed by **Liam Neeson**

The Weaver Thief Husband written and performed by **Harrison Ford**

The Weaver Thief Wife written by **Melissa Mathison** and performed by **Rita Wilson**

The Spinning Wheel written and performed by **Angela Lansbury**

The Imperial Dresser written and performed by **Nathan Lane**

The Dresser's Spectacles written and performed by **Jason Alexander**

The Imperial Physician written and performed by **Dr. Ruth Westheimer**

The Empress written and performed by **Madonna**

The Imperial Ladies-in-Waiting written and performed by **Carrie Fisher & Penny Marshall**

The Imperial Princess written and performed by **Melissa Joan Hart**

The Imperial Prince written and performed by **Jonathan Taylor Thomas**

The Imperial Wizard written and performed by **Jeff Goldblum**

The Holy Man written and performed by **Dan Aykroyd**

The Court Jester written and performed by **Robin Williams**

The Imperial Mirror written and performed by **Geena Davis**

The Emperor's Underwear written and performed by **Calvin Klein**

The Imperial Throne written and performed by **Rosie O'Donnell**

The Heralding Horn written and performed by **Fran Drescher**

The Honest Boy's Mother written and performed by **Joan Rivers**

The Honest Boy written and performed by **Steven Spielberg**

The Imperial General written and performed by **Gen. H. Norman Schwarzkopf**

The Emperor written and performed by **John Lithgow**

The Moth written by **Karen Kushell** and performed by **Jay Leno**

Produced and directed by André Mika

Engineered by Jeff Sheridan at Soundworks, Los Angeles, California
Musical score by Stan Xidas, Xidas Music, Chicago, Illinois
Vocal score composed by Greg Jasperse
Music engineered by Scott Reandeau

Additional dialogue recorded at The Warehouse, New York, New York
Engineered by Billy Eric

Senior producer for *The Emperor's New Clothes* project is Karen Kushell.

VERY SPECIAL PEOPLE, WITHOUT WHOM THE AUDIO PORTION OF THE PROJECT WOULD NOT HAVE BEEN POSSIBLE:

Lisa St. Amand, Bonnie Herman, Bob Bowker, Jennifer Shelton, Dr. Stephen Zegree, Bob Lizik, Craig McCreary, Jim Hines, Christin Foley, Piper-Lori Parker, Andrew Jasperse, Elizabeth Bright, John Rodgers, Ryan Billington, Roger and Lynn Tallman, Michael Charzuk, Xidas Music/Chicago, Prism Recording/Los Angeles, Soundworks/Los Angeles, Ron Rose Productions, Inc., DreamWorks International Productions, Western Michigan University School of Music, Peter Stougaard, Charles Herrera, Michael Duff, Chris Cameron, and Jami Mika